For Elizabeth Edwards

PRESIDENT

ROSEMARY WELLS

SCHOLASTIC PRESS ◆ NEW YORK

SCHOOL ELECTION!

"I want to win!" said Charles to his mama and daddy.
"We're on your team!" said his mama.
"We'll make sure it happens," said Charles's dad.

IT WAS ELECTION TIME at Barkadelphia School.

"Whoever collects fifty paw prints can run for president of the school," announced Miss Kibbler.

"I wonder who will win," Otto said to his best friend, Melanie.

"Tiffany will win!" shouted all the popular kids.
"Tiffany's the cutest and the smartest!"

"I want to be president!" said Tiffany to her mother and father.
"You're the most popular girl in the fifth grade, dear," they said.
"We'll help you win the election! No problem!"

"Charles! Charles! Charles!" shouted all the sports bugs.
"Charles is the captain of all the teams!"

VOTE STRONG!
VOTE CHARLES!

VOTE CUTE VOTE TIF!

Expensive signs went up all over Barkadelphia School. Real bumper stickers were stuck on lockers.

By the end of the first day, Tiffany and Charles had already collected their paw prints.

Preferred Seating in the Cafeteria! VOTE TIFFANY!

Soda in the Water Fountains! VOTE CHARLES!

Tiffany's mother persuaded the school cheerleaders to shout out a "Tails Wag for Tiffany" cheer.

Charles's dad hired a famous glee club to sing the "Bulldog" fight song at Barkadelphia School football games.

"Wow," said Otto. "They are on a roll."

"I don't know why they are so popular," said Melanie.

"They don't care about anybody but themselves!"

Suddenly, Otto had an idea.
"I'm going to run for president," he said.
He began by asking his classmates what they really wanted at Barkadelphia School.

"Who cares for more meat at lunch?
I want watermelon in the cafeteria,"
said Berty.

"Forget skateboards in the hall, a homework help line is what I need," said Martha.

"I'd like five minutes of beautiful music every morning," said Bettina.

"How about bigger towels in the gym showers?" suggested Boris.

"A class trip to the Madison Square Garden Dog Show would be a big motivator!" said Carlos.

"Our school band needs a set of bongo drums!" added Peter.

Charles's dad beefed up their campaign.

"Whoppo Burgers and shakes? That'll be the day," said Melanie.

"No fair!" cried Tiffany.
"I'm going to lose!
I can hardly breathe!"

"We are way smarter than Charles,"
said Tiffany's best friends, Ashleigh
and Jasmine.

The next morning, Post-it notes appeared on all the lockers.

"Not true! I've never cheated!" growled Charles.
"No worries!" said Charles's best buddies, Mike and Bucky.

Mysterious flyers appeared in the cafeteria that afternoon.

Tiffany had a meltdown.
"Not true! It's all lies!" she sobbed.
"We'll fix his wagon," said Ashleigh and Jasmine.

CHARLES CHEATS!

CHARLES CHEATS!

CHARLES CHEATS!

Flashing buttons popped up the very next day.

"You're not going to be done in by a bunch of buttons," said Mike and Bucky.

Overnight, a huge banner appeared on one wall of the gym.

TIFFANY WRONG on hair spray! WRONG For Barkadelphia School!

Meanwhile, Otto collected his fifty paw prints, one by one.
One by one, he listened to everyone in the school, even the
kindergartners. They wanted blankets at nap time.

"Now I need some campaign cookies," said Otto.
"We'll make them together," said Melanie.

On election eve, Charles's dad hosted a Whoppo Burger pep rally.
"I want to thank you all in advance for voting for me!" said Charles.
"I am a born leader!"

Everybody got in line to vote.

"I'm crossing my fingers!" said Otto.
"And I'm crossing my toes!" said Melanie.

Tiffany's mother arranged for a pancake breakfast on election morning.
"It's going to be me!" said Tiffany. "Me! Me! Me!"
Otto just passed out his cookies.

Miss Kibbler counted the ballots. She asked Mr. Muzzle, the
school principal, to recount them. Finally, the results were in.

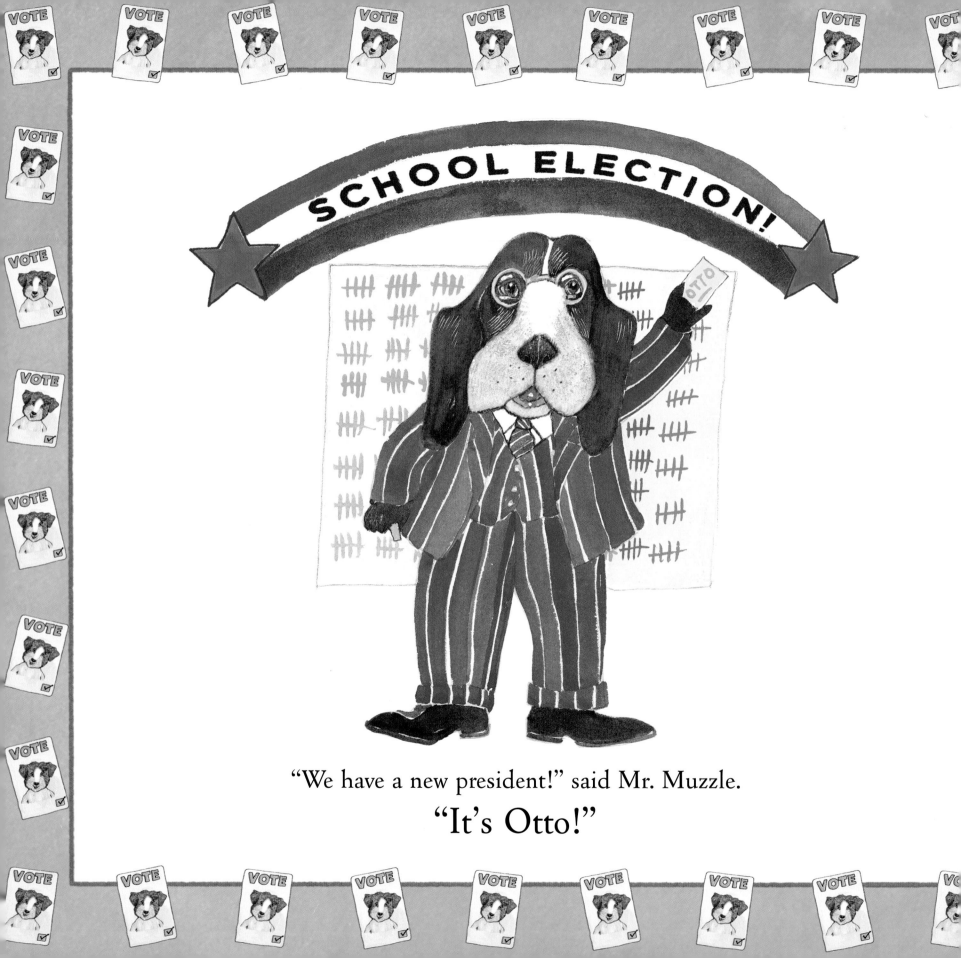

"We have a new president!" said Mr. Muzzle.
"It's Otto!"

Everyone cheered, especially the kindergartners.

"Wait 'til next year, buddy!" said Charles's dad.

"Barkadelphia School is just a little blip, my treasure," said Tiffany's mother. "You will win paws down in junior high!"

"It's watermelon day in the cafeteria, the nap-time blankets just arrived for the kindergartners, and we have the Madison Square Garden Dog Show," said Otto. "It's hard work being president!"

"Let's bake up more cookies," said Melanie.
"Enough for everyone!"

Library of Congress Cataloging-in-Publication Data Available
ISBN-13: 978-0-545-03722-8

ISBN-10: 0-545-03722-0

12 11 10 9 8 7 6 5 4 3 2 1   08 09 10 11 12 13/0
Printed in Singapore   46   First edition, May 2008

This book was set in 20-point Cloister Old Style.
Book design by Elizabeth B. Parisi
Hand lettering by Rosemary Wells, Michael Syrquin,
and Elizabeth B. Parisi